LOOK OUT FOR THE WHOLE SERIES!

Case Files 11 & 12: The Case of the Medieval Meathead & The Case of the Messy Mucked Up Masterpiece

Case Files 13 & 14: The Case of the Guy Who Makes You Act Like a Chicken & The Case of the Felon with Frosty Fingers

Case Files 15 & 16: The Case of the Bogus Banknotes & The Case of Eight Arms and No Fingerprints

Case Files 17 & 18: The Case of the Flowers That Make Your Body All Wobbly & The Case of the Guy Who Looks Pretty Good for a 2000 Year-Old

Case Files 19 & 20: The Case of the Gobbling Goop & The Case of the Surfer Dude Who's Truly Rude

Case Files 21 & 22: The Case of the Cactus, the Coot, and the Cowboy Boot & The Case of the Seal Who Gets All Up In Your Face

Case Files 23 & 24: The Case of the Snow, the Glow, and the Oh, No! & The Case of the Fish That Flew the Coop

THE CASE OF THE
BOGUS BANKNOTES

*Hodder
Children's
Books*

A division of Hachette Children's Books

Special thanks to Lucy Courtenay and Artful Doodlers

Copyright © 2008 Chorion Rights Limited, a Chorion company

First published in Great Britain in 2008 by Hodder Children's Books

2

A Catalogue record for this book is available from the British Library

ISBN 978 0 340 97085 0

Typeset in Weiss by Avon DataSet Ltd,
Bidford on Avon, Warwickshire

Printed in Great Britain by
Clays Ltd, St Ives plc

The paper and board used in this paperback by Hodder Children's
Books are natural recyclable products made from wood grown in
sustainable forests. The manufacturing processes conform to the
environmental regulations of the country of origin.

Hodder Children's Books
a division of Hachette Children's Books
338 Euston Road, London NW1 3BH
An Hachette Livre UK Company
www.hachettelivre.co.uk

Chapter One

Birds twittered happily in the trees overhead as the Five hiked uphill through cool green woodland. They were carrying backpacks with supplies for lunch.

"I don't have anything *against* picnics," Dylan grumbled to the others as he pushed his glasses up his nose. "But I just don't think you should have to hike somewhere to eat."

Max shifted his backpack to a comfier position and blew his shaggy blond fringe out of his eyes. "But then you're hungrier when you get there, so you can eat more," he pointed out.

"Oooh – compelling argument," Dylan said,

completely diverted. "Objection withdrawn. Let's hike for several days, and I'll eat an entire all-you-can-eat buffet."

Jo, the most sensible of the Kirrin cousins, rolled her eyes at the boys. "It won't take several days to get to Havenglen Valley," she said. "It's right over this ridge."

Allie paused and looked around at the dappled light and shade, the scampering squirrels in the treetops and the gorgeous views through the woodland. "I have to say," she told the others, "it's – *très gelato!*"

Her French accent made two squirrels wince and race away from the path. Jo, Dylan and Max looked confused. Even Timmy lifted an eyebrow.

"Why did you just say 'very ice cream' in a mix of French and Italian?" Jo asked.

Allie looked cross. "I meant 'very pretty'!" she said. "No wonder I'm flunking French. I thought it'd be easy – I'm great at French fashion and perfume and food—"

"Then they give you the old switcheroo and make it about the French *language*," Dylan put in sympathetically. "Sneaky."

"You meant *très jolie*," Jo told Allie kindly as they moved through the trees and reached the top of the ridge. "Havenglen Valley *is* really pretty. It's green, it's full of butterflies, it's . . ."

Her voice tailed away as the Five stopped on the crest and stared down into the valley. The valley's edges were still green and lush. But in the centre, everything was decaying. Trees were stunted and dead, leaves lay shrivelled and brown and there was no more birdsong.

"Ohh," Jo gasped, clapping her hands to her mouth. "It's a disaster area!"

Chapter Two

The cousins scrambled down from the ridge and made their way into the heart of the dying valley. They tried to understand what they were seeing.

Dylan touched the brown leaves of a nearby bush. They crumbled to nothing. "I'm no expert," he told the others, staring at his dusty fingers, "but unless this is the rare Brown Crumbly Dustbush, something seems to be wrong."

"I don't know what's going on here," Jo said. "But we're going to find out what caused this."

Timmy nudged a shrivelled brown fern with his nose. It collapsed in a cloud of dust, making Timmy sneeze.

"*Quel fromage!*" Allie said, staring at the scene of devastation.

"You just said 'what cheese'," Jo told her as kindly as she could. "I think you meant *quel dommage* – 'what a shame'."

"How come you know French?" Max said, looking impressed. "Have you been living in Paris when we're not looking?"

"I spent a summer in French Guiana with Mum, collecting plants," Jo explained.

"Did you get many?" Max asked.

"Plants, no," Jo told her cousin, scratching herself at the memory of French Guiana. "Mosquito bites, yes."

"Speaking of Aunt George and plants, let's take her some samples," Dylan suggested, pushing up his sleeves. "Maybe she can work this out."

Following Dylan's example, the others pushed up their sleeves too. Everyone set to work, trying to gather plants. Half of what they picked turned to dust as soon as they touched it. It was hard going.

Finding the end of a vine plant, Max picked it up. He followed it, pulling it up like a long rope and coiling it over his arm as he went. He was so intent on the vine that he didn't notice a small track. Until a jeep almost drove straight over him with a honk and a skid.

A dark-haired outdoorsy guy flung open the jeep door and hopped out.

"Sorry," said Max, looking shocked by his near-death experience. "I forgot to look both ways before following a vine on a forest path."

"Hope I didn't scare you," boomed the dark-haired stranger. He held out his hand. "Rory O'Riordan. I came up here to paint some landscapes." He waved his other arm around as if it held a paintbrush. "Paint, paint, paint," he explained, pointing at the easel, canvases and other paint supplies sticking up out of the back of his Jeep.

"Hope you brought plenty of brown," Jo said.

Rory O'Riordan frowned. "Indeed," he said, glancing around. "I'd heard it was pretty here. I guess I'll drive further up the valley." He gave another cheery mime, pulling his hands up and down. "Drive, drive, drive!"

"Odd guy," Dylan told Max in a low voice. "Odd, odd, odd."

"Good luck," Allie told the stranger. "I hope it's prettier up the valley."

"Well," said Rory O'Riordan, "as Van Gogh would say . . ." He paused. "Actually, I don't know what he would say – I don't speak Dutch," he confessed, and roared at his own joke. "Ha ha – I'm off! Off, off, off!"

"Bye, bye, bye," said the Kirrins automatically, looking at each other as Rory O'Riordan leaped back into his jeep, started the engine and sped away.

"He could've started by painting all these plants," Dylan said, waving around. *"Plants with Brown Crumbly Dustbush* would look much better green."

Chapter Three

Two hours later, the Kirrins staggered down the drive towards Jo's house. They each carried an armful of plant samples from Havenglen Valley. Max had excelled himself, and was carrying a small tree.

"Maybe it's some kind of pesticide . . ." Jo told Dylan as they rounded the corner of the house

"Or a bug," Dylan offered, shifting his armful of plants before he dropped them. "Some kind of tree-killing bug . . ."

A timid-looking seventeen-year-old waiting by the front door leaped to his feet as the Kirrins approached.

"A bug?!" he squealed, hopping up and down and batting at his clothes and head. "Where?! Is it in my hair?! Get it off me!!"

The Kirrins gawped as the teenager pulled a bottle of insect repellent out of his pocket and squirted it madly around himself, coughing and spluttering at the smell.

"Does anyone recognize him?" Dylan checked, frowning.

The others shook their heads.

"Nope . . ." Allie said.

"Good," said Dylan, sounding relieved. "I was afraid we were friends with a complete loon."

The teenager stopped jumping around. He smoothed down his clothes and looked a little sheepish. "Cyril. Cyril Butterby," he said, introducing himself. "I was contacted by Allie's parents to tutor her in French." He cleared his throat, before saying in flawless French: *"Je m'appelle Cyril."*

"Oh!" Allie said, her eyes widening as she took in her geeky new tutor. "Well, I guess I need all the help I can get. Um . . . *Jam apple Allie.*"

"Looks like you've got your work cut out," Jo told

Cyril sympathetically. "I'm Jo, this is Timmy, Dylan . . . that tree over there is Max."

She indicated the small tree that was now waving at Cyril and saying: "Hello! . . ."

"So, when does this French tutoring start?" Allie asked, brightly.

"*J'ai été engagé pour vous enseigner le français et les cours commencent dès maintenant,*" said Cyril.

Allie's expression didn't change.

"That means 'now'," Jo translated.

"Oh," said Allie, her face falling. "What's French for 'Aw, stink!'?"

"Hey," said the small tree suddenly. "There's bees in here. Shoo!"

As he shook the tree, Max overbalanced. He toppled sideways to land with a thump on the ground. "Woaahh – oooof," he grunted. "Timber . . ."

A bee bumbled out of the tree. It was heading straight for Cyril.

"Bees?" Cyril said in panic. "Where? They sting!" He swatted at the buzzing bee. "Go away!"

When the bee ignored him, Cyril started running away. He leaped over the porch railings, swerved around a flowerbed and hurdled the woodpile in his hurry to escape.

"Wow," said Max, watching Cyril in admiration. "I bet he'd make a pretty good athletics coach, too."

Cyril was now pelting across the lawn. He jumped over a bench and smacked face-first into a tree. "Oooff . . ."

Max looked disappointed. "Maybe not . . ." he said, as Cyril slid to the ground in a heap.

When Cyril came round, the Kirrins showed him into the house. Before long, he had set himself up in the study with Allie. Allie sat at the desk with a thick textbook of verbs open in front of her. She looked depressed.

"*Aller* – to go," Cyril explained. He held up a picture of a drinking fountain. "I go to the germ-filled drinking fountain . . ." he said, raising his eyebrows encouragingly at Allie.

"*Je . . . vais . . .* to . . . *la* fountain *de* drink," Allie struggled.

Cyril sighed and tried another picture. This time, it showed a hospital. "I go to the hospital to be tested for every possible germ . . ."

Allie took a deep breath. "Je . . . *vais* . . . to . . . *el* house *des le* people for curing."

The study door opened.

"Good," said Jo, as she and the others peered inside. "You're learning 'to go'. Beause that's what we've got to do."

"But we're in the middle of a verb drill!" Cyril spluttered as Allie eagerly pushed back her chair.

"Perfect," said Max, waving a manual drill in the air. "We've got some drilling in mind, too!"

"Aunt George found poison in the plant samples," Dylan told Allie.

"Someone's *poisoning* Havenglen!" Jo said, sounding outraged. "We're going to check the soil for contamination."

Max looked at his drill. "Well, *Jo* wants to check the soil," he said. *"I'm* just excited about making holes."

Allie closed her book with a snap and jumped up to join the others.

"But we're supposed to study four hours a day!" Cyril wailed. "Allie's parents might yell at me! Yelling gives me a rash!"

Jo shrugged. "So come with us," she suggested.

Cyril's eyes boggled. "Outdoors?" he said. "I'm allergic to outdoors! There are germs, and things that bite and sting and crawl up your nose."

"I can fix that," Max offered. Pulling a clothes peg out of his pocket, he popped it on to Cyril's nose.

"If I becub a victib of nature, I'll be upset . . ." Cyril told them, a little nasally.

"Well, *c'est la vie!*" Jo said.

Allie looked puzzled. "You want me to say *'la vie'*?" she asked. "OK: *la vie!*"

Jo looked at her cousin. "You do need to study," she said at last. "That is very clear . . ."

Chapter Four

Back at Havenglen Valley, the devastation was worse than the Five remembered. Max pulled his drill from his pocket, stuck the end into the soil and started cranking the handle. Jo and Dylan watched.

Allie and Cyril stood together lower down the hillside. In a large broad-brimmed hat hung with mosquito netting, Cyril looked as if he was off to explore the Amazonian rainforest. Instead, he was still trying to tutor Allie.

"To resume – verbs," said Cyril, batting nervously at his mosquito netting as he checked the air for insects. "Repeat after m— wa . . . ah . . . ah . . . ah-CHOOO!!!"

His sneeze nearly blew him off his feet.

"Wa-ah-ah-chooo!" Allie repeated dutifully. She looked pleased. "Hey, I sneezed in French!"

Cyril sneezed again – and again – and again. "A-CHOO! A-CHOO! A-CHOO! A-CHOO!" Each sneeze threw him into the air, doubling him over every time.

The Kirrins stopped their soil sampling to watch the entertainment until Allie's tutor finally stopped sneezing. Still catching his breath, Cyril spotted a butterfly on a nearby tree limb.

"B-B-Butterfly!" Cyril squealed in terror as the insect fluttered towards him. "Get me out of here!"

He jumped away from the butterfly, crashing straight into a tree. This time, it was the tree that fell over.

"Oohhhhhh," Cyril groaned as the tree toppled over, showing its withered and diseased roots.

"He *really* doesn't like the outdoors," Max said, shaking his head. "He keeps head-butting trees."

Jo bent down to examine the broken-off roots. "These roots can't even hold the tree up," she said. "If every tree's like this, the topsoil could become unstable."

The Five looked at the ground beneath their feet. The valley sides sloped steeply downwards.

"That's not good, right?" Dylan said uneasily.

Jo moved away from the tree. "In extreme cases," she began, "unstable topsoil can lead to a . . ."

There was a feeling of movement. A second tree fell over, and a third. Allie and Cyril looked alarmed as the ground shook beneath their feet. So did Max and Dylan, who finished Jo's sentence for her:

". . . LANDSLIDE!"

Max and Dylan dropped out of sight. A tide of brown earth and uprooted trees slid after them,

down the hill – down, down, down . . .

"Whoahhhhh!" Max and Dylan yelled. They climbed aboard a passing tree trunk. Hurtling downwards, they started trying to ride it like a surfboard.

"Come on!" Jo yelled. She started to run after the boys. After a split-second, Allie and Timmy followed.

Max and Dylan were getting the hang of tree-surfing. They passed Cyril, who was tumbling downhill in the middle of a bush. Angling themselves slightly, the boys leaned to the left, steering towards Allie's hapless tutor.

"Cyril – grab hold," Dylan yelled over the wind. "We'll give you a ride!"

"What?!" Cyril shrieked, clinging on to his bush. "I could never—"

A branch on Max and Dylan's surfing tree snagged Cyril's trouser leg, upended him and dragged him helplessly behind them. They thundered on down the hill.

"Woahhhh!" Cyril wailed as dirt and stones and twigs whacked him in the face. "This is why nature is the worst thing in the world!"

Still on a firm footing, Jo, Timmy and Allie raced ahead of the sliding tree. "Timmy, grab that vine!" Jo shouted, leaping and bounding down the slope.

Timmy pulled a long vine over to Jo, who handed one end to Allie. "We can use the vine to help stop the boys!" she explained, sprinting across the path of the careering log and pulling her end of the plant rope tight.

The tree trunk hit the vine square on.

"Ha!" Allie shouted in triumph, clinging on to her end of the vine as the tree trunk catapulted upwards and the boys flew through the air.

"WOOAAAH!"

Cyril ended up in the middle of a tree. Max and Dylan were luckier – if a heap of mud and muck can be called lucky.

"Yeuchhhhh!" they shouted as dark brown goo splattered them from top to toe.

"Sorry," Jo panted, sprinting up. "That didn't exactly go to plan."

"It's all right," Dylan gasped, wiping mud off his face. "At least we got the soil samples we need."

"Allie," Max asked, wringing goo out of his hair. "Did you ever find out the French for 'Aw, stink'?"

Cyril fell out of his tree with a squelch, straight into Max and Dylan's mucky puddle. He pulled the world's smallest white handkerchief from his pocket and tried to dab the mud away. It was like trying to clean up a cowpat with a feather. "It's *'zut, alors'!*" he muttered, dabbing away. "And I couldn't agree more."

Back at Jo's house, Allie was stuck in the study once again, looking even more depressed than before. Her French textbook lay open on the desk in front of her.

"From now on," Cyril announced, "all study will take place *indoors*."

He pulled out an assortment of drops, and put them in his eyes, ears and nose. Then he gave himself a blast with some mouth spray. "Where no bacteria can jump on you," he continued, clicking the lid on to his mouth spray with some force, "and set up house with all their little baby bacteria, bacteria shopping centres and—"

"I get it, I get it," Allie interrupted crossly. "But—"

"No buts," Cyril said at once. "Havenglen is

very dangerous. Repeat after me – *Havenglen est très dangereux.*"

Allie sighed. *"Havenglen est très dangereux,"* she repeated. *"Havenglen est très dangereux . . ."*

In the distance, unnoticed, the brown of Havenglen Valley was starting to spread. It was heading for Falcongate.

Chapter Five

A new day, a new French challenge. Allie sat at the desk in the study again, facing the window. This time, she looked almost pleased to be there.

"Today we'll be doing vocabulary," Cedric announced, carrying a pair of headphones into the room. "Well, *you'll* be doing vocabulary," he amended, setting the headphones down on the desk. "I'll be making cream of radish soup. Prevents rickets."

"Don't want rickets . . ." Allie murmured in agreement.

Cyril headed for the door. On his way, he pointed to a small videocamera sitting on a high bookshelf. "But that camera will let me see what's going on in here at all times," he reminded Allie. "Happy studying!"

Allie put the headphones on. She pressed "play" on a CD player sitting on the desk and settled down to work.

"Where is the library?" she repeated obediently. *"Oooo esss la baybleeeooootayke?"*

The door banged open. Max and Dylan sauntered in, looking innocent.

"So," Max said loudly. "Where is that book with all the, you know, really interesting stuff in it?"

Dylan went over to a shelf and pulled out a book. He held it up. "Why, here it is!" he announced.

In the kitchen, Cyril was stirring soup. He glanced at his video monitor as he added pepper, just in time to see Max and Dylan poring over a book in front of the camera, making loud noises of interest and completely obscuring the rest of the study.

Thinking nothing of it, Cyril turned back to his soup and tasted it. It needed chives.

With Cyril's view blocked, the Five got to work.

Carrying the torso from a dressmaker's dummy, Jo entered the study and hurried over to Allie. Allie swiftly pulled off her headphones, and Jo replaced her in the desk chair with the dummy. Then she took a balloon from her pocket and started blowing it up.

"Look at that!" Dylan said loudly, pointing at the book for Cyril's sake and shuffling a teensy bit closer to the video monitor. "How very interesting!"

Jo clipped the inflated balloon to the top of the dummy as quickly as she could. Pulling open a desk drawer, Allie found a wig and slapped it on top of the balloon. The headphones followed, plus a spritz of perfume.

"I *always* wear Black Rose," Allie whispered by way of explanation.

Jo sighed. She would never understand her American cousin. Hunting in her pocket, she took out a CD and replaced it with the one in the CD player. Allie's recorded voice spilled into the room.

"*Luh cheeeeyen est tray jolleeee. Luh cheeeyen est tray jolleeee . . .*"

The switch completed, Jo led Allie past Max and Dylan and out of the study.

"Well," said Max breezily to the camera, "that's enough interesting stuff. Time to go!"

In the kitchen, Cyril was adding salt to his soup. He glanced at the monitor, to see Dylan and Max leaving the study. A figure sat at the desk, headphones on, its back to the camera. *"Luh cheeeeyen est tray jolleeee"* parroted through the monitor.

"That's *le chien est très joli!*" Cyril called out, correcting his pupil. "I have to go to the shop for more vegetables . . ." He picked up the TV monitor, adding: "But I'll be keeping my eye on you!"

The cousins ran past the kitchen window behind him, giggling.

The Kirrins walked down the main street in Falcongate. Jo pulled the ziplock bag containing the Havenglen soil sample out of her bag.

"Mum doesn't have the equipment to test soil," she explained to the others. "She says the agricultural lab can test our samples."

Ahead of them, a familiar-looking jeep was parked up against the pavement. Rory O'Riordan stepped out of the art-supply shop, his view obscured by the stack of huge tins in his arms.

"Hi, Rory!" Dylan said, stopping. He checked out Rory's tins. "That's a lot of turpentine. You must have a lot of paint brushes to clean. Or one big brush the size of Belgium!"

"I'm out in the field for weeks at a time," Rory explained, hefting his tins a little higher. "So I stock up whenever I'm in town. Stock, stock, stock!"

The kids offered to help load the turpentine into the jeep. But while they were loading, a peculiar figure bounded into view. It was Al Fresco Freddy, Falcongate's most colourful character. Even by Freddy's standards, he was looking extra colourful today.

"Woooh – look out!" roared Freddy. "Here comes Freddy!"

He bounded right into the midst of the Kirrins on an extraordinary pair of jumping stilts. Everyone stepped back in alarm, and Jo dropped the soil sample bag.

"Watch it!"

"Hey!"

"Look out!"

"Woahhh . . ."

Balancing precariously on his stilts, Freddy was

wearing an enormous gold medallion and at least five or six expensive watches up each arm.

"I'm a very rich man," Freddy announced, bouncing up and down. "Lots to do! No time to talk! Got to go!"

He started off with a tremendous leap, landing smack on Jo's sample bag and popping it. The Havenglen soil scattered across the pavement as he sprang away.

"Where would Al Fresco Freddy get all that bling?" Allie asked in admiration.

"And where did he get those awesome jumping stilts?" Max demanded. "I'd give my right leg for a pair of those." He paused. "But then I couldn't use them. Huh."

Something was fluttering down on the pavement. Dylan bent down and picked it up. It was a fifty-pound note.

"Fifty pounds!" Dylan gasped. "Did Freddy get a job modelling for *Goofball Gazette*?"

Jo was sitting down on the road, holding up the empty, torn remains of the ziplock bag. "Freddy will have to wait," she sighed. Timmy licked her consolingly on the cheek. "We've got to go back to

Havenglen and get a fresh soil sample."

Allie glanced across the road. Cyril was leaving the greengrocer's, carrying two bunches of radishes.

"It's Cyril!" Allie hissed in alarm. "If he gets home before us, he'll find a dummy in my seat!"

"There'll be a dummy in your seat either way," Dylan quipped. He held up his hands and grinned. "Didn't mean it, just had to say it."

The kids looked at each other. How were they going to get back to Jo's house before Allie's tutor?

Chapter Six

Timmy started barking at a truck parked along the street. An old mattress lay in the back, with springs poking out of it at odd angles.

Two minutes later, Dylan was lashing two mattress springs to his feet with strips of the mattress fabric. The others were already bobbing up and down on the pavement, testing out their own improvised jumping stilts.

"OK, let's spring into action!" Jo grinned. "See? I *can* be funny."

She leaped over a nearby fence. The others followed. Bounding from one garden to the next, they raced home, dodging laundry and frightening

a flock of sheep in the lane that led back to Jo's house. Dylan got carried away, and leaped higher than the others – disappearing into the canopy of an overhanging tree and disturbing an angry bird or two.

At last, they reached Jo's garden. With magnificent accuracy, Allie sprang through the open study window, followed by Timmy. Max, Jo and Dylan jumped on round to the back of the house – just as Cyril steered his bicycle up the drive.

Allie kicked the dummy under the desk, making

its balloon head float up to the ceiling. She swiftly popped the balloon with a well-aimed nail file, and slipped into the desk chair. The wig fell neatly on to Timmy as Cyril put his head around the study door.

"Hi, Cyril," Allie said innocently. "Or should I say *bon . . . joveee*?"

"Woof," said Timmy, from underneath the wig. It kind of suited him.

Max had made it into the kitchen. He bounded round like an enthusiastic kangaroo. "These are brilliant! I'm never taking them off!" he announced, before adding: "Ouch" as his head hit the ceiling.

Jo and Dylan came in behind him. Taking off their stilts, Jo and Dylan peered closely at the fifty-pound note Freddy had dropped.

"This is counterfeit," Dylan said.

Jo frowned. "You sure? It looks fine to me."

"Hello?" Dylan reminded her. "It's *money* — my favourite thing in the world. See the windows in the building behind the historical-looking bloke?"

Jo looked a little closer.

"There's three," Dylan explained. "There should only be two."

Max bounced past. "To Al Fresco Freddy's – follow me!" he shouted, before slamming into the ceiling again. "Owwww!"

Being a colourful individual, Al Fresco Freddy had no ordinary address. He lived in the upturned hull of an old boat, which sat in the middle of a small clearing in the woods. In the fading evening light, piles of luxury goods could be seen round the front door: plasma screen TVs, computers, paintings, exercise equipment and a jet-ski, among other things.

"Hmmm," said Max, looking around. "Freddy isn't around . . ."

Allie looked at her tutor. He was wearing safety goggles, a sterile mask and rubber gloves. "Are you performing surgery later, Cyril?" she asked.

"If you're ever going to speak French—" Cyril began, his mouth muffled by the mask.

"Which is doubtful," Dylan put in cheerfully.

"—I have to tutor you every minute," Cyril continued. "Since you insist on roaming outdoors, I have no choice but to protect myself."

"OK," Allie sighed. She looked fierce as she

added: "But I go to the bathroom *alone*."

Dylan checked out Freddy's loot. "Last time we visited Freddy, he owned half a tin of boot polish and an upside-down oil can to sit on," he said, stroking the jet-ski.

"So where's he getting the counterfeit money?" Jo asked, frowning.

Timmy sniffed the air, then put his nose to the ground.

"What can you smell, Timmy?" Jo said, looking alert. "Show us . . ."

The Kirrins and Cyril followed Timmy as he trotted to the edge of the clearing and vanished between the trees. They pushed through the undergrowth, Cyril complaining and being shushed by the others. At last, they came to another clearing, where a spring was welling up through the ground and a pool had formed.

Jo pushed the others back behind a bush. Al Fresco Freddy was kneeling by the edge of the pool.

"O, Spirit of the Magic Pool, grant me thy damp money, that I may acquire a caravan, a microwave, a monkey in a dinner jacket and a lifetime supply of chicken gravy," Freddy intoned.

32

He stuck his hands into the water and pulled out a huge handful of soaking wet fifty-pound notes. Holding up the notes in the moonlight, Freddy shouted with glee. Then he scuttled off, tucking the money into his trousers.

The Five and Cyril crept out of the bush.

"Phew!" said Max, sniffing the air and grimacing. "There's an odd smell . . ."

"Well, Freddy has been known to wear malt vinegar as cologne," Jo pointed out.

A clump of banknotes was still bobbing in the water. Dylan scooped them up. It was time to head for home.

"Yes, this is definitely counterfeit as well," Dylan announced, as the cousins stood in the study back at Jo's house a little later and looked closely at the dripping wet notes. "We should take it to the police."

Jo shook her head. "No good. Tonight's Constable Stubblefield's limbo class."

The Five winced, imagining the large lady police officer in full tropical outfit, limboing under a stick to the sound of steel drums.

"Which means she'll be at the chiropractor all day tomorrow," Jo said.

The banknotes were dripping water on Allie's exercise book. "Hey – my assignment!!" Allie said in dismay, snatching up the book.

Dylan took the money and wrung it out over a potted plant near the window. Timmy sniffed the pot and made a face.

Taking his cue from Timmy, Dylan sniffed the cash. "Hey," he said. "It wasn't Freddy who smelled odd – it was the *money*!"

"Let's not jump to conclusions," Max advised. "They could both smell odd."

"So, the money smells because the water smelled . . . ?" said Allie, looking confused.

Jo found a map and spread it out where the others could see it.

"Freddy lives on one side of this hill," Max said, tracing the map with his finger. "On the other side is the southern end of Havenglen Valley!"

"Freddy's 'magic pool' was fed by a spring," said Jo, thinking the problem through. "If that spring was fed by an underground river, it would mean the water is poisoning the valley!"

They all turned and looked at the potted plant near the window. It had wilted and died already.

"So who's making this fake money – and where?" Dylan asked.

The Five exchanged looks. Somehow, they *had* to find out.

Chapter Seven

Back at Havenglen the following morning, the Five pored over the map that Jo had brought with her. It showed a lake at the north end of the valley.

"The underground river would run from this lake all the way to Falcongate," said Jo, tracing the river along the map. "It's heading right towards our house!"

"So if you're right, everything from here to there is poisoned," said Dylan. "But . . ."

Jo lowered the map. The kids stared at the long Havenglen lake down in the heart of the valley. It glinted clear and blue in the morning sunlight.

"For a poisoned lake, it looks awfully clear and

blue," Max said, echoing Dylan's thoughts.

"*Bleu!*" Allie said brightly.

Max gestured around. "And the vegetation about here is still pretty green."

"*Vert!*" put in Allie. "See, I've been studying!"

Standing just behind Allie, Cyril nodded. "And I bathed in mosquito repellent, so I'm cleared for action!" he said happily. "This mystery stuff is exciting!"

"*Excitant!*" Allie said in triumph.

"The source of the poison has to be somewhere between here and the dead area," Dylan said. "But where?"

The sound of a jeep engine rumbled in the distance. The Five hurried over to a rock that jutted out over the valley, and looked down. Rory O'Riordan was driving towards them.

"Hey, painter man!" Max called, waving his arms. "Where you going? Going, going, going?"

The jeep screeched to a halt. "I'm painting a series of watercolours of the devastation," said Rory, leaning out of the window. "Paint, paint, paint."

"That ought to make a nice Christmas card," Dylan said politely.

Rory O'Riordan waved a hairy arm at them. "I'll be camping in the area awhile," he said, revving the engine. "Good job I picked up plenty of turpentine. Ha, ha – see you! Bye, bye, bye!"

Rory drove away in a cloud of dust. The kids watched him go.

"He said he's painting *watercolours?*" Jo said thoughtfully. "You don't use turpentine to clean watercolour brushes. That's for oil paint."

Allie looked surprised. "But why would he lie about painting?" she said.

"Maybe he's not here to paint . . ." said Dylan, tapping his nose.

"So what *is* he doing here?" Max asked.

The kids looked at each other.

"I don't know," Jo said at last. "But something about this doesn't smell right."

"It might be my anti-fungal cream," Cyril suggested.

Jo shook her head. "There's something very wrong," she said. "Let's go and find out what it is."

The kids headed after Rory O'Riordan's jeep. It had left a dusty trail, and was easy to follow. At last they found it, parked below a low cliff overlooking the valley. Timmy took a cautious sniff. The cousins hung back, unsure what to do next.

"Why would he just leave his truck in the middle of nowhere?" Jo asked.

"Because if you leave it in a car park, someone always bashes your wing mirror," said Dylan sadly.

"There are footprints going up the bluff . . ." Max said, staring at the rock above them. He scrambled up hand over hand, until he reached the top. "Come on up!" he called down to the others. "You've got to see this!"

The other Kirrins and Cyril struggled up the bluff after Max. Reaching the top, they took in the view. It looked as if someone had taken an enormous ruler and drawn a long line across the valley, dividing the green land from the brown.

"It's like there's a line between what's alive and what's dying," Jo said, shading her eyes from the sun as she looked down at the devastation.

Timmy barked and began sniffing the ground.

"Timmy smells something," Dylan said, looking round. "Maybe he's picked up Rory's scent."

"He's found more than that!" shouted Cyril,

hurrying after Timmy. "He's found a . . ."

Cyril suddenly disappeared. The Kirrins heard one word echoing back at them.

". . . ho-o-o-o-ole!"

There was a thud.

"Ooof," came Cyril's echoey voice from somewhere under the ground. "*Aidez-moi!*"

"That means: 'Help'!" said Allie in delight. "Hey, I'm getting pretty good at this!"

The Five ran to the hole. Max leaned cautiously over the edge. "Cyril, are you OK?" he called down.

Cyril looked up at Max's face. He looked more cheerful than Max had ever seen him. "I'm bruised and I'm dirty, and I'm loving it!" he grinned. "If you could just throw me down a rope, I could . . ."

The four cousins and Timmy jumped down the hole.

"Or you could come down here to me . . ." said Cyril, looking a little surprised.

Chapter Eight

The Five and Cyril moved stealthily along the bank of an underground river. They were passing through a dramatic twilight world of stalagmites and stalactites. The sound of dripping was starting to get annoying.

"Underground river . . . present," Dylan said, stopping and glancing around. "Source of poison . . . ?"

Up ahead, the tunnel opened into a cavern. The cavern glowed with electric light, and the thump of machinery was beginning to drown out the dripping.

"It's not exactly a big neon sign saying 'Answer

This Way', but it's close!" Max grinned.

The cavern was humming with people and equipment. An electric generator powered two huge printing presses, which were spewing out banknotes. Vast piles of blank paper lay stacked on wooden pallets. Gigantic drums of ink were stacked into pyramids, and a long workbench held engraving plates and cans of chemicals. Workers bustled from the presses to the workbench and back again.

"It's a counterfeit operation," Dylan whispered to the others as they all hid near the mouth of the cavern. "I mean, it's a *real* operation, but . . ."

". . . the money they're printing isn't real," Max put in, helping his cousin out.

"Well, it's real," said Allie, "it's not *imaginary* – but it's . . ."

"It's counterfeit money!" Jo interrupted impatiently. "They're printing counterfeit money!"

"And they use the turpentine to clean off the press," Dylan said, watching as one of the workers tossed the contents of a large can of turpentine over the printing plates.

As the engraver threw the empty can aside, another worker emptied the dregs of a chemical can straight into the underground river. The river was greenish-grey, bubbling with noxious fumes that formed into bubbles, floated up and popped against the tree roots growing down through the cavern roof.

"The printing chemicals are poisoning the river," Jo gasped, watching as the bubbles rose and popped and did their deadly work. "That's what's killing the valley."

"And all for money," said Dylan, shaking his head. "They're giving money a bad name."

Rory O'Riordan walked in through another entrance across the cavern from the Kirrins. He approached one of the printers.

"How's the replacement run coming along?" he said abruptly.

"Nearly ready," the printer replied. "I had to stay up three nights in a row to print off the new batch of notes."

"That'll teach you to drop a pallet of fifty-pound notes into the river," Rory O'Riordan snarled.

"Those notes must have come up in Al Fresco Freddy's 'magic pool'," Max guessed, craning his neck for a better view into the cavern.

"Now he won't get his caravan," said Allie, sadly. "Too bad – I could see him driving along, microwaving . . ."

"We need some photographic evidence," Jo said, watching the scene. "Pass me your phone, Allie."

Allie handed Jo her phone. Jo dropped to her belly and started to worm her way towards the printing presses. Copying Jo, the others followed. Timmy and Cyril brought up the rear.

Cyril had almost caught up with the others when his foot snagged in the power cable snaking across the cave floor. He tried to jerk his leg free – and plunged the entire cavern into darkness as he pulled the cable from its socket in the electric generator.

"Ooops!" Cyril gasped as the counterfeiters shouted with surprise and alarm. "My fault. I'll fix it."

"No!" Jo hissed, wriggling around. "Cyril! Wait—"

The lights came up to reveal Cyril standing by the generator, one hand still holding the power cable. The counterfeiters stared at the invaders in shock. Within moments, they had surrounded the Kirrins. Still on their hands and knees, the Five peered up at a circle of unfriendly faces.

"*Zut, alors!*" said Allie weakly.

Chapter Nine

There was no escape. The counterfeiters hustled them to their feet and marched them down to line up along the bank of the underground river. Rory O'Riordan stared at the invaders in outrage.

"Wherever I went, there you were!" he said, stabbing a finger at the Five. "You couldn't just leave things alone. Alone, alone, alone."

"Not when your operation's poisoning the whole valley!" Jo shouted defiantly.

"When we're finished here, we'll buy a new valley . . ." Rory O'Riordan growled. "Though I think I'll buy it somewhere warmer." He turned to his men. "Throw 'em in the river," he said with a

46

nasty grin. "Splash, splash, splash."

As Rory O'Riordan's henchmen stepped forward to obey their boss, the surface of the river began bubbling frantically. Then it exploded upwards. Al Fresco Freddy zoomed into view with an underwater scooter. He was dressed in a wetsuit, and had an aqualung strapped to his back. As he broke the surface, he pulled out the aqualung's mouthpiece.

"My magic pool ran out of money!" he shouted crossly. "I came up to find if there was any more. I've booked an expensive singles cruise!"

Jo thought quickly. She pointed at a stack of banknotes. "There's more of your money there, Freddy!" she shouted. "Go and grab it!"

"Don't let him get it!" Rory O'Riordan screamed as Al Fresco Freddy scrambled ashore with his eyes gleaming. "No, no, no!"

The Kirrins made the most of the distraction. They broke away from their captors and dodged off through the printing presses and stacks of paper. A counterfeiter advanced on Jo, but Timmy jumped out from behind a pile of turpentine cans and bit him on the bottom.

"Owwwwwww!" howled the man, clutching his shredded trousers and trying to hide the clowns printed on his boxer shorts.

While Allie threw cans of turpentine at her pursuers, Freddy tried to pocket more fake notes. Dylan ran past him, seizing the abandoned sea-scooter.

"Don't blow it all in one place, Freddy!" Dylan shouted gleefully, turning the scooter round and firing up the propeller, which he aimed at the stacks of counterfeit notes. The fake money blew through the air like a smelly snowstorm. Rory and his men stopped chasing the Kirrins and started chasing the money instead.

"Ready, Cyril?" Max said, standing beside a pyramid of ink barrels.

Cyril nodded. They hurled themselves against a barrel at the bottom of the pyramid and started rocking it.

"Achhh – strained a ligament," Cyril gasped.

Despite Cyril's injury, their efforts paid off. Like a house of cards, the rest of the barrels came tumbling down. Barrels bounced everywhere, springing leaks and spraying ink in all directions. The counterfeiters scattered, trying not to get squashed. Blue, red, green – Rory O'Riordan's henchmen turned all the colours of the rainbow as they slipped and slid in the gloopy mess. Seizing their moment, the Kirrins and Cyril fled.

In hot pursuit Rory O'Riordan raced out of the cavern with his henchmen. One of the counterfeiters pointed. Cyril was limping along behind the Five, crying: "Wait for me! I've got a stone in my *chaussure!*"

"Get him!" Rory roared. "He'll lead us to the others. Others, others, others!"

Jo and her cousins stood on the overhanging rock above Rory O'Riordan, surrounded by shrivelled, dead trees.

"And here we are!" Jo said merrily.

They pushed at the rotten trees. Dead roots tore out of the ground. The trees toppled over and tumbled down the slope, knocking over the counterfeiters like skittles and trapping them beneath heavy branches.

The Kirrins slid down the bluff and ran over to where the villains lay groaning beneath the dead foliage.

"Pretty good catch, huh?" said Max, looking satisfied.

Jo snapped her phone shut. "Constable Stubblefield's on her way," she told the others. "She says Freddy won't be in trouble – he just has to give back the stuff he bought."

A beaming Cyril came over to join them.

"Nice play-acting, Cyril!" Dylan said, clapping Allie's tutor on the back. " 'I've got a stone in my *chaussure*'!"

"That means shoe!" Allie sang.

Rory O'Riordan groaned. He struggled to get up

from under the tree pinning him down.

Allie stepped smartly up to him. *"Et ne bougez pas jusqu'à ce que la police arrive,"* she snapped.

Cyril looked delighted. "Allie, you just said: 'Don't move until the police get here' in perfect French!" he gasped.

"Wow," said Allie, looking stunned. "It just spilled right out of me."

"Then I think my work here is done," Cyril said.

"Erm, Cyril," Jo said carefully. "You've got a spider on your neck."

Cyril's eyes widened. "I have?" With an effort, he controlled himself. "I don't care!" he announced.

"Then I guess our work here is done, too," Allie grinned.

As the Five shook hands all round, Cyril started twitching. "Although now it's climbed down my back, and I can't quite deal with that . . ." he muttered a little helplessly, reaching for his back with a hop and a grimace.

The Five watched Cyril jiving on the spot for a moment.

"He might also make a very good dance teacher, if we ever needed lessons," Dylan observed.

Epilogue

Back at Jo's house the following day, the Five were filming the next of their Top Tips.

"Sticky Situation Number Fifty," Jo announced from behind the camera. "You Have To Spot Counterfeit Money."

Max and Allie sat at the desk. A row of bank notes lay in front of them.

"There are lots of ways to detect counterfeit notes," Max began. "For instance, counterfeit notes tend to be very floppy . . ." He held up one of the notes. It drooped sadly.

"Or you can hold it up to the light – that should show a watermark on a real note." Allie continued, demonstrating.

"And a magnifying glass will show if the small details look sharp," Max added. "Counterfeit notes will be blurry."

Allie smiled brightly at the camera. "And there's our own personal method, the Dylanometer," she said.

Jo panned the camera round as Allie carried a note across to Dylan, who sat blindfolded in a chair. She handed him the note. He took a sniff.

"A Swiss twenty-franc note," Dylan said at once. "Printed in 2002." He took the note from Allie's fingers and pocketed it. "Thanks, Allie."

Allie started after him. "Hey, that's mine!" she said crossly, reaching for the note.

Dylan dangled the note out of his cousin's reach. "Using the Dylanometer is expensive," he shrugged.

CAN'T GET ENOUGH OF THE FAMOUS 5?

Then continue your adventure online to play games, meet the gang, learn cool tips and tricks, watch videos, grab downloads and more.

Check out www.famous5.co.uk NOW!

Read the adventures of George and the
original Famous Five in

THE
FAMOUS FIVE'S
SURVIVAL GUIDE

Packed with useful information on surviving outdoors and solving mysteries, here is the one mystery that the Famous Five never managed to solve. See if you can follow the trail to discover the location of the priceless Royal Dragon of Siam.

The perfect book for all fans of mystery, adventure and the Famous Five!

ISBN 9780340970836

LOOK OUT FOR THE WHOLE SERIES!

THE CASE OF EIGHT ARMS
AND NO FINGERPRINTS

Hodder
Children's
Books

A division of Hachette Children's Books

Special thanks to Lucy Courtenay
and Artful Doodlers

First published in Great Britain in 2008 by Hodder Children's Books

2

A Catalogue record for this book is available from the British Library

ISBN 978 0 340 97085 0

Typeset in Weiss by Avon DataSet Ltd,
Bidford on Avon, Warwickshire

Printed in Great Britain by
Clays Ltd, St Ives plc

The paper and board used in this paperback by Hodder Children's
Books are natural recyclable products made from wood grown in
sustainable forests. The manufacturing processes conform to the
environmental regulations of the country of origin.

Hodder Children's Books
a division of Hachette Children's Books
338 Euston Road, London NW1 3BH
An Hachette Livre UK Company
www.hachettelivre.co.uk

Chapter One

The water was teeming with life.

A huge sea turtle swam past a fat-faced grouper. Codfish and manta rays flicked their tails through fronds of seaweed. And a full-size plastic deep-sea diver goggled at a plastic treasure chest amid the ruins of a lost (plastic) civilization.

The crowd stared through the glass into the Seaview Aquarium's enormous water tank. There were gasps as a vast octopus floated past the viewing window. Its body was the size of a large dog, and its eight tentacles floated behind it like fat ropes.

The evening queue to see the octopus trailed

right away from the aquarium. It snaked past the ice-cream stand, the brightly lit penguin enclosure and the toilets. It ended in a mountain of stuffed animals, balloons and aquarium pennants.

"How long have we been in this queue?" Dylan demanded, from his position beside the stuffed-animal mountain.

"It seems like forever," Jo sighed. She kicked at the ground with her scuffed trainers.

Max leaned back against the wall. "It'll be worth it to see the giant octopus," he said. "Did you know they can change colour depending on their mood?"

"My nose itches and I can't reach it," said the stuffed-animal mountain. It sounded remarkably like Allie. "Could someone scratch it for me?"

Dylan took the claw of a big, cuddly lobster in Allie's arms and turned it to scratch his cousin's nose for her. Allie sighed with relief.

"Helpful *and* cute," Jo grinned, stroking her dog Timmy's head. "Not you, Dylan – the toy lobster."

Max was still thinking about the octopus. "Octopuses can be red and then purple?" he said, frowning at his information leaflet. "How do they do it?" He squinted, shut his eyes and

started waving his arms around like an octopus, pulling horrible faces. "See?" he gasped at last, opening his eyes again. "No colours – I only get a pain in my neck."

"It's not just *your* neck," Jo teased her cousin.

"I could go home happy right now," Allie said, shifting her armful of aquarium goodies so she could pull out her mobile. She started scrolling through her photos. "I've seen all the cute animals they have here – cute penguins, cute seals, cute dolphins, cute guy who feeds the dolphins . . ."

The queue started to move.

"Finally!" Max said in triumph. "It's octopus time!"

Suddenly, all the lights gave a flicker and fizzed out. The whole park was plunged into darkness.

"We apologize," came a nasal voice through the loudspeaker, "but due to a power failure, Seaview Aquarium is temporarily closed. We welcome you back tomorrow."

"What?!" Max roared. "That's ridiculous!"

"Try to light up bright red with anger," Dylan suggested, squinting around in the darkness. "I can't see a thing."

Jo fumbled in her backpack and produced a

torch. "That's because there's no moon tonight," she said, switching it on.

"Well," Max sighed, reaching across to borrow Jo's torch so he could make a couple of octopus shadows on the wall. "Like they said, we can come back and see the octopus tomorrow."

Inside the dark water tank, the octopus swam on. A scuba diver slid into view. Out of nowhere, a net rippled out and snared the eight-legged monster. Turning red with rage, the octopus struggled, squirting jets of black ink at its attacker. But it was useless. Trussed up and helpless, the octopus was dragged from its watery home.

Chapter Two

The four Kirrin cousins and Timmy were back the following day. The park had only just opened, and there was hardly anyone around.

"See?" said Max, leading the others towards the big water tank. "It's worth getting up early to be first to see the octopus."

"Good morning," burbled the loudspeaker over the cousins' heads. "We apologize, but the octopus is not available for viewing today."

Sighing, the Five turned round and started heading away from the aquarium again.

"I'm beginning to hate that loudspeaker," Max grumbled.

"They should warn people when the octopus is out for dry-cleaning, or polishing, or whatever it is they do with an octopus," Allie said earnestly as they passed the viewing deck for the water tank.

Dylan suddenly stopped. His glasses almost slid off his nose. "Shh!" he said. "Listen – I hear money! The clink of coins in a collecting tin." Money was Dylan's passion. He cocked his head. "Ten pence," he said, listening carefully. "No – fifty!"

Up on the viewing deck, a large pink starfish was

dancing around an awestruck audience of kids. A couple of the smaller children tried to copy the costumed performer's dance moves.

Dylan whistled. "Look at the money he's making," he said, staring at the dancer's cash collection on the ground.

"Everyone loves a dancer," Allie said with a shrug. "Even a starfish, if it's funky enough."

Max started grooving with the starfish and the little kids.

"What a great way to get rich!" Dylan gasped. "I'll invent a new dance, get famous and the money will start to flow . . ."

The others watched as an expression of bliss passed over Dylan's face. They knew their cousin well enough to recognize the signs. Dylan was in the grip of a cash fantasy.

"Step one," Dylan murmured, briskly pulling himself out of his daydream. "Come up with a dance."

He tried a few experimental dance moves, before slipping on a pool of black liquid that lay on the deck. "Wooaah – oof . . ."

"When the money starts flowing in, you'd better

save it for some bandages!" Jo laughed, helping Dylan back on to his feet.

Timmy sniffed at the black liquid on the ground. He barked.

"What is this stuff?" said Allie, bending down and looking at the dark stain.

"It's like ink," said Jo. She glanced round. "It's all over the deck and the sides of the tank."

"I bet it's octopus ink!" Max said suddenly. "As if somebody wrestled an octopus on to the deck. Or else the world's biggest fountain pen exploded."

A pleasant, rather fragile-looking aquarium employee stepped up on to the deck behind them. "I'm afraid that's exactly what happened," she sighed, looking at the mess. "Oh, dear."

"Just my luck," Max groaned, clapping his hands to his unruly blond head. "I missed the world's biggest fountain pen exploding."

"No, it was the octopus," the woman assured him. She held out her hand. "I'm Sara Pilcher, Director of Marine Biology."

Jo took Sara's hand and shook it. "I'm Jo," she said. She waved around at the others. "This is Timmy, and these are my cousins."

"Oh, you're George's daughter!" Sara exclaimed, looking at Jo with interest. "Your mother helped us with some of our marine plants. How is she?"

"Oh, you know," Jo said pleasantly. "Odd."

"That's nice," said Sara, nodding. "Anyway, when we opened this morning, Octie was missing."

"Octie?" Dylan repeated.

Sara looked shy. "I've named all the animals," she explained. "Snaily, Coddy, Eely."

"Let me guess," Dylan said. "A snail, a cod and an eel. Those are *great* names."

Brrinngg! Brrinngg!

Sara fumbled with her mobile. "Oh, I have to answer this," she said, checking the screen. "Sharky's calling."

Allie's eyes widened. "A *shark* is calling you?"

"No, Dr Leon Sharky, my chiropodist," said Sara, moving away to take the call. "My feet are killing me – ohhhhh . . ."

The cousins looked at each other. A missing octopus sounded like a case for the Famous Five!

"Well," said Jo into the silence. "The trail of ink leads that way . . ."

Chapter Three

They took off after the line of inky blotches.

"So it looks like the fishnapper hoisted Octie out of the tank . . ." Jo said, following the line of splashes.

"But the blotches alternate every few feet, so they didn't just walk . . ." Dylan added.

Sure enough, the pattern of blotches changed. There was a big splodge, suggesting a fight of some kind – then a single inky tyre track that wiggled off and out of sight.

"Hey look!" Max gasped, pointing at the tyre track. "Octie escaped on a unicycle!"

"Or . . ." Dylan clicked his fingers to make the

thoughts come quicker – ". . . maybe the fishnapper loaded Octie into a wheelbarrow . . ."

They followed the snaky line through the park to the covered outdoor cafeteria. The single tyre track turned into a huge circle of ink splattered across the floor like a massive spin picture.

"But then how did this circle of ink get everywhere . . . ?" Allie asked in confusion.

"You might be right about the wheelbarrow," Max told Dylan, "but I'm sticking with the unicycle."

Humouring Max, the others tried to picture an octopus on a unicycle.

"Octie was trying to get away from the fishnapper . . ." Max continued, his brain hurting with the effort, "and he grabbed that ceiling fan . . ."

The others followed Max's pointing finger up to the fan on the ceiling.

"Then it let go and was flung on to that flagpole . . ." Jo continued, getting into Max's theory.

The cousins ran out of the cafeteria, following Jo towards the flagpole near the centre of the park.

"But the poor thing couldn't hold on, and he fell . . ." Allie said, stopping at the foot of the flagpole.

Everyone looked at the inky outline of a scuba diver at their feet. It looked like the octopus had squashed his captor. Weirdly, Max's theory made sense.

More ink blotches stretched off towards the back fence of the park. They ended at an exit gate, which was marked with a large red X in a circle.

"And then the fishnapper took Octie out through that gate," Max concluded triumphantly. His theories didn't work that often. He was determined to enjoy the moment.

". . . I've got to go, Dr Sharky," Sara said, her phone still to her ear as she followed the Five. "I'll just soak my feet and see you tomorrow." She clicked her phone off. "That's the employees' gate," she said, following the cousins' gaze. "They're the only ones with the entry code."

BEEEP.

The gate buzzed and opened from the far side. A tall, military-looking fifty-year-old man in grey trousers and a blue blazer stepped through, a

walkie-talkie strapped to his belt.

"Gate's clean, Miss Pilcher," he barked. "No fingerprints." His eyes swept professionally over the Kirrins. "I don't know these people," he said at once. Pulling out a metal-detector wand, he waved it in front of the Five. "All right, they're clean," he said, a little reluctantly.

Sara made some introductions. "Kids, this is Mr Gilley. He's our Chief of Park Security."

Jo's eyes lit up. "Ooh – have you questioned the employees?" she asked eagerly.

"Have you contacted Constable Stubblefield?" Dylan asked at the same time.

"Of course," Mr Gilley said. "The result . . ." He snapped open his phone, punched a number and held it up for everyone to hear.

"Constable Stubblefield is on holiday," Constable Stubblefield's tinny voice informed them. "If you are a criminal, do not commit a crime. If you have committed a crime, please put yourself in jail. Thank you."

Gilley snapped his phone shut again. He did everything with military precision. "As for the employees, I personally screen all of them," he said.

13

"I don't believe any of them would steal an octopus."

"And yet, Octie is outtie," Allie pointed out.

"I expect someone hacked the . . ." Mr Gilley stopped and stared at Dylan, who was gyrating and bopping on the spot. "What is that boy doing?" he demanded. "Is there something wrong with him?"

"He's coming up with a new dance craze," Jo explained.

"I see," said Mr Gilley coldly. "Stop it. And I suggest you children leave this investigation to the professionals. Good day."

He waved his metal-detector wand at them again, just to make a point. Then he marched away.

Chapter Four

"Since when do we leave investigations to someone else?" Jo said crossly, as the Five ate lunch at the cafeteria. "I think we should question the park employees."

"And *I* think I made a mistake ordering fish and chips," Max said. He looked queasily at his plate. "I hope I'm not eating anyone who used to live here."

"And *I* think I've got my dance craze," Dylan announced. "Allie – hit it . . ."

Allie was a girl of many talents. Beat-boxing was perhaps the most surprising. As Dylan put down his hat, threw some notes in it to encourage others and broke into a loose-limbed dance, Allie started

making some crazy noises.

"Boomp-boomp-*cha*-tss-tss-tss-tss-ooh—"
Allie began. She shot a glance at Jo. "Could we
question the animal trainer first? Buh-doo-doo-
doomp . . . I want to see the penguins again.
Boomp-boomp-cha . . ."

A little girl who was passing by stopped dead.
She stared at Dylan, entranced.

"Look, Daddy – that boy has no bones!" she
cried. "I'll give him some money for medicine."

She dropped a coin in Dylan's hat, and left.

Dylan shrugged. "Well, fifty pence is fifty
pence . . ." Still dancing, he bent down to pick up
the money while Allie kept right on beat-boxing.

The Five mooched round the park for the rest of the
day, questioning employees about the missing
octopus and getting no answers. Every now and
again, Dylan would set up pitch and Allie would
beat-box again. Soon Dylan had collected seventy-
three pence and a bottle top. It was time to rethink
his dancing ambitions.

The Five headed for the small amphitheatre
in the centre of the park. They stood and watched

for a bit as a short, curly-haired animal trainer called Vernon Squelch showed a red ball to a plump seal sitting on the stage in the centre of the amphitheatre.

"I'm afraid I don't have time for questions," Squelch squeaked. "I have to conduct the animals' training session."

He rolled the ball towards the seal.

"Hey!" he said, slowly and loudly. "Balance that ball on your nose! Hey! Seal! You! On your nose! The ball! Balance it!"

Unimpressed, the seal gave a fishy belch and stayed exactly where he was.

"Did you ever consider *showing* your animals what you want them to do?" Jo suggested to the sweating trainer.

Timmy pawed at the red ball. Knocking it expertly into the air, he caught and balanced it on his nose. Then he tossed it to the watching seal, who caught it on his own nose.

"Then you reward them with a fish," Max said, picking up the fish bucket and holding a fish out to the trainer.

Vernon Squelch screamed and leaped into Allie's arms. "You do it!" he blubbered. "I'm terrified of fish!"

"Could you get over it?" Allie grunted, staggering beneath Squelch's weight. "'Cos you're kind of heavy."

"Just answer a few questions, and the mackerel goes back in the bucket," said Jo.

The trainer knew when he was beaten. "I don't really know anything about the missing octopus," he panted. "But I did see a strange car in the car park last night."

"'Strange' as in it was hovering and glowing and piloted by a three-headed space monster?" Max checked, swinging the mackerel thoughtfully between finger and thumb.

"No," said Vernon Squelch, looking increasingly sweaty. " 'Strange' as in 'I've never seen it before'."

Max sighed. "Shame," he said.

"It had an odd bumper sticker," Squelch went on. "I don't remember if it said anything, but . . ."

Whatever the trainer had been going to say was forgotten. Marine mammals appeared on every side: penguins, seals, even a walrus. They scurried through the amphitheatre, waddling up and down the steps and making the kind of racket they usually saved for a polar-bear attack.

"Hey – someone let the animals out!" Allie gasped.

Chapter Five

"I'll handle this," said Squelch importantly. "I work with animals. You – penguin!" he shouted. "Get back in your cage! Go! I mean it! Hup!"

The penguin kept waddling in the opposite direction. Marine animals were streaming from all sides, flooding through the park like a honking, roaring, stinky swarm of bees.

"Timmy!" Allie shouted. "Help me with the penguins!"

Timmy herded the penguins expertly towards Allie. Allie waddled off, copying the way the penguins moved. Impressed, the penguins followed her to a nearby ice-cream van. Jo flicked open the

van's back door, ushering the happy penguins into the enormous freezer at the back.

A seal flumped through the crowd, barking loudly. Terrified park visitors fled before the mass of blubber.

"Hey, boy – catch!" Max tossed the red ball at the seal, who stopped chasing a screaming woman in order to catch the ball on his nose. Other seals flumped in to join the game. Soon they had a passing thing going to rival any basketball team.

One enormous elephant seal was sitting in the middle of a flowerbed, bellowing its lungs out. Jo surprised it by bellowing straight back. The elephant seal stared at her. Then it swayed out of the flowerbed as fast as its blubber would allow, following Jo through the park.

"BWAAAAH!" it roared. "BWAAAA!"

Still bellowing back, Jo led the seal up to the big water tank. She stepped aside at the last moment. The elephant seal flopped straight into the tank, sending up a huge wave that soaked Jo from head to foot.

"Heyyyy!" Jo leaped aside and tried to wring herself dry. The elephant seal heaved itself out of

the water with a fish in its mouth. It gave the fish lovingly to Jo.

"Erm . . . thanks," said Jo warily.

"I think a certain elephant seal has a crush on a certain Jo," Allie grinned, watching as the elephant seal smothered Jo with fishy kisses.

As Jo giggled and tried to push the seal away, a long tentacle snaked out of the tank and wrapped itself around Jo's fish.

"Hey – a tentacle!" Max said, pointing as the tentacle withdrew to the tank again, still clinging to its prize. "That means . . ."

The Five raced up to the plate-glass viewing wall, where Sara Pilcher and Mr Gilley stood looking into the tank. The large octopus swam gracefully into view, and away again through the weeds.

". . . Octie is back!" Max cheered.

"Obviously someone let the penguins and the seals and the whatnots loose to create a distraction, and then they put the octopus back in the tank," said Mr Gilley.

"There's just one problem," said Sara. She slowly turned to face the Five. "Now Mr Turtley the sea turtle is missing!"

* * *

The next day, the cousins returned to the aquarium. This time, they'd brought their scuba diving gear with them. They were going to look at the crime scene for themselves.

"These are just kids," Mr Gilley spluttered at Sara. "Why are they going into the tank? The octopus is back – it seems someone's just playing pranks on us."

"They're brilliant at solving mysteries," Sara said admiringly. "Maybe they can get an idea of where Mr Turtley went."

"And you never know," said Dylan as he wriggled into his wetsuit. "Underwater dancing might be the next big thing." He paused. "Oooh . . . the 'Deepsea Dylan' . . ." He began another dance, building in a few swimming actions plus some superhero moves. "It's a winner!" he said, punching the air and leaping into the tank with a splash.

"There's something very odd about that boy," Mr Gilley muttered as the others followed Dylan into the water.

The four cousins swam among the fish, plants and rocks, studying them. The tank was so huge

that it was almost like swimming in the open sea.

The octopus came up to investigate the tank's new visitors. It held its tentacle out to Max. Max shook it. Pleased, the octopus held out another tentacle. Max shook that one as well, wondering how long this was going to take.

Jo swam off along the wall of the tank. She spotted something glittering on the sandy floor of the tank, and ducked down to pick it up. A gate slid open noiselessly above her. A blunt white nose poked through. And an enormous shark swept into the tank with a flick of its powerful tail.

Chapter Six

Out on the deck, Timmy saw the shark first. He barked a warning. But the glass walls of the tank were too thick, and Jo didn't hear him. She had reached the glittering something on the tank floor. She held it up in the watery blue light. It was a gold tie-pin.

The shark swam towards Jo. Timmy barked again more urgently. The shark swung its tail and hit Jo as if she was a cricket ball. Jo dropped the tie-pin in surprise, catching it again just before it sank out of sight among the water weeds.

Max, Allie and Dylan had noticed Timmy going crazy on the other side of the glass. They spotted

the shark. Seizing the tails of a passing shoal of groupers, they let the groupers tow them towards Jo. As they swept past the plastic deep-sea diver, Max and Allie let go of their fishy rides and yanked it out of the ground. Max pulled out the diver's bubble-effect air hose and directed the jet of bubbles at the shark's belly as it swooped on Jo. The shark rolled over and away from its prey.

Jo quickly joined the others, and they swam for the surface. But the shark had already recovered. It swam after them with hard, sweeping movements of its tail and opened its mouth wide . . . just as the kids scrambled out of the tank and collapsed safely on the deck.

Sara, Mr Gilley and Timmy helped to yank the cousins away from the water's edge. Looking irritable, the shark swam away.

"All right, that was no prank," Mr Gilley admitted. "That gate is on an automatic timer so the shark tank can be cleaned at night."

"So someone deliberately altered the timer," Dylan gasped, lying back on the deck and catching his breath.

"It might have something to do with this . . ."

said Jo. She held up the golden object she'd retrieved. "It's a tie-pin – I found it at the bottom of the tank."

"Sara," Allie said earnestly, "this might not be the kind of thing people would notice, but has anyone in a suit and tie been swimming in your tank lately?"

Five minutes later, they were in Mr Gilley's office: a small room with a desk, a filing cabinet and a few security monitors. Mr Gilley loaded a video tape.

"Well, just the other day, a guest fell into the tank . . ." Sara explained.

A picture flickered into focus on the monitor. It showed a thin, nervous-looking man in a suit, standing on the deck of the big water tank. He was clutching a bag tightly to his chest.

"What's that in his hand?" Jo asked, peering closely at the bag.

"A computer memory stick . . ." said Dylan.

In the background, two young boys were playing tag. They ran past the man. One boy dodged behind him, the other tried to tag his friend – and pushed the man into straight into the tank.

The man flailed around in the water. The

octopus swam up and gave him a friendly tickle with a tentacle, before the turtle swam underneath him and pushed him up to the deck. Huffing and puffing, the man struggled out of the tank with a clam clinging to his bottom.

Dylan burst out laughing as the hapless man on the screen prised off the clam and flung it back into the tank. "Hee, hee – clam," he gasped, holding his sides. "That's why, no matter what, television will always be the best thing in the world."

The man was now patting his pockets, searching for something. Looking upset, he hurried off the screen, leaving a trail of water behind him.

"Looks like he lost something," said Allie.

"He definitely lost his dignity – and that can be hard to regain," Max smirked.

Jo's eyes widened. "He doesn't have that memory stick any more!" she said. "I bet he dropped it in the tank and he's trying to get it back."

Dylan turned to the security man. "Mr Gilley, have you looked at the security tapes of the night the octopus was stolen?" he said.

"No tapes – the power was out," said Mr Gilley promptly. "I've looked at last night's tape when the

turtle was grabbed – doesn't show a thing."

Jo held up the tie-pin. "So this is all we have to go on . . ." she said.

Engraved with a star and the mysterious letters "A.T.", the tie-pin twinkled in the bright office light.

Chapter Seven

The starburst logo glowed on the computer screen. They were back at Jo's house, and Dylan was on to something.

"This is the website for something called Tiberius Tech," he said, his fingers flying over the keyboard while the others gathered round. A newspaper page flicked up on the screen. "And this is the newspaper from last week."

Looking interested, Allie leaned in closer. "Eeeww – does it have my horoscope?" she said eagerly. "I want to find out what happened."

Jo read out the small print on the screen. "Micro-technology pioneer Tiberius Tech reported the

theft of a new system which allows remote control of shipping . . ."

"Hmmmm," said Dylan thoughtfully. He clicked back to the starburst logo screen. "Website again . . ."

A little hourglass whirred on the screen.

"Welcome to Tiberius Tech," came a computerized voice. "Dangerous technology for a dangerous world."

"Kind of a gloomy website," Allie said as the muted colours swirled around the screen. "They should have flowers or smiley faces in the background."

"Along with our Radar Ionizer, our developing Ship Shifter promises to re-shape the world's naval fleets," continued the computer.

On the screen, a little burst of animation showed a battleship cruising along on the ocean.

"See? Now that's cute," said Allie, looking pleased.

"Smart public relations," said Dylan. "They make destructive technology, but this shows people they also have a heart."

The computer voice was still talking.

"Imagine if *you* could take control of a ship from the comfort of your own home."

The cartoon battleship cruised up on to a beach, up the side of a mountain and into a volcano crater at the top. After a moment, the volcano erupted, blasting the ship into the stratosphere.

Allie sighed. "And, back to gloomy . . ."

"I bet Tie-Pin Man is the one who stole the technology," said Dylan, manoeuvring the cursor on the screen. "I bet that's what's on the memory stick."

"Maybe he thinks one of the fish in the tank swallowed it, so he's snatching them to see if he can find it," Max guessed.

"Well, we'd better find it first," said Dylan. "Otherwise . . ." He clicked on to the website again, replaying the animation. They watched the battleship climb up the mountain and blast into space one more time.

"Not just gloomy," said Allie into the silence as the others looked at each other. "Scary."

Back at the aquarium, the Five found Sara on the edge of the big tank, tossing small fish from a

bucket into the water. The cousins stepped in to help. Even Timmy joined in, grabbing fish from the bucket with his teeth and throwing them into the tank.

"There you go, Eely," said Sara as the various creatures swam up to grab some lunch. "Octie. Swordfishy."

"Let me guess," said Jo as a grouper swam into view. "The grouper fish is named Groupery."

"No, the grouper is named 'Sir Isaac Newton'," Sara explained. "He looked just like a 'Sir Isaac Newton' to me."

Allie took hold of a fish. "Here ya go, Sir Isaac—"

As she went to throw the fish into the tank, it suddenly squirmed out of her hands. It shot through the air and straight down the back of Dylan's shirt.

"Waahhggg!" Dylan screamed.

He leaped to his feet, wriggling and squirming and thrashing his arms like a crazed robot. His hat fell to the ground. Timmy eyed Dylan carefully before backing away to a safer distance.

"Well, there's your new dance craze!" Max grinned. "Here – I'll video you so you don't forget it."

"Make sure to show the people in the background bopping along!" Allie called as Max pulled Dylan's camera from his rucksack and filmed Dylan as he grooved helplessly around the deck.

"Hey, that's a good idea!" Jo said suddenly. "Not the dance-craze-bopping-along thing – that's so absurd it's sad . . ."

"Then what?" Max demanded. He cocked his head. "What's cookin' up in Jo-town?"

Jo snapped her fingers. Her eyes were bright.

"We should check the security tape from last night – we might see Tie-Pin Man in the background somewhere," she said.

Max caught on. "So even if it doesn't show the turtle theft, we'd at least know if Tie-Pin Man was here."

"Hey – what about me?" Dylan squealed, still wriggling to escape the fish as the others started away.

"Oh, sorry . . ." said Jo, stopping just long enough to drop a coin in Dylan's hat.

Chapter Eight

"I've already *told* you," snapped Mr Gilley as the Five crowded into his office again. "I watched the tapes."

"But did you look for the Tie-Pin Man earlier in the day?" Jo pressed. "We just want to see if he was here."

"And if maybe he looks like the agent of a government in league with space aliens," Max said earnestly.

The others looked perplexed. Max shrugged. "You can usually tell from the way they comb their hair," he explained, in case it helped.

"Oh, for pity's sake . . ." Mr Gilley grabbed a video and shoved it into the player. A picture

appeared on the monitor. The security man started fast-forwarding through the footage. "As you can see, no Tie-Pin Man . . ."

"Wait," said Allie. "Show that again."

Dylan looked alert. "Why – did you see something?"

"No, but people look funny in fast motion," Allie explained, giggling. "Like penguins." She started doing a penguin impression, moving around the room at speed. "Doe-dee-doe-dee-doe . . ."

Mr Gilley pressed another button. The video returned to normal speed as day turned to night on the screen. "And then we reach last night . . ." he said.

On the monitor, the big water tank lay quietly in the darkness, a full moon reflected in the rippling water.

"And since you're all such clever, observant children," said Mr Gilley ultra-sarcastically, "you'll notice THERE'S NOTHING GOING ON."

"Well, thank you for your time, Mr Gilley," said Jo quietly. "You're quite right – there's nothing going on." She looked at her cousins. "Come on, let's go."

The others exchanged puzzled looks as Jo left Mr Gilley's office. Obediently, they followed her outside. Timmy gravely shook paws with Mr Gilley and brought up the rear.

"That wasn't like you at all, Jo," said Allie in wonder as they walked back outside.

"Yes, you were polite and agreeable," said Max. He looked confused.

Jo whirled round to them. "Keep quiet and listen to me," she snapped, putting her hands on her hips.

Max looked relieved. "There," he said, happy things were back to normal. "That's our Jo."

"I don't know what he's up to, but Gilley's lying to us," Jo said. "That tape he showed us wasn't from last night."

Dylan frowned. "How do you know?"

"There was a full moon reflected in the water." Jo explained, stroking Timmy.

Allie caught on. "And there's been no moon at all the past few nights," she gasped. "That's why it's been dark. Apart from being night time, I mean."

"Gilley doesn't want us to know what goes on here at night," Jo said. She looked thoughtful. "So I think we'll have to see for ourselves . . ."

Back at the aquarium that night, Mr Gilley paced up and down the viewing deck beside the big water tank. Everything was dark, quiet and deserted.

The man who they had watched falling in to the tank walked nervously into view.

"You're late!" Mr Gilley snapped.

"Oh, sorry," said Tie-Pin Man, looking down. The sea turtle was plodding along at the end of a lead in his hand. "This turtle is really quite slow."

Mr Gilley paced up and down as the Tie-Pin Man and the turtle got a little closer. Then a little closer again.

Mr Gilley's patience snapped. "Oh, for the love of . . ." He hurried up to the turtle and heaved it into his arms. Staggering slightly, he then wove his way back to the tank. The turtle turned its large green head and started chewing Mr Gilley's hair.

"He likes to eat hair," said the Tie-Pin Man as Mr Gilley tipped the turtle into the tank and cursed, clutching at the place where a hank of hair had been torn out of his scalp. "That's why I didn't carry him." He glanced down into the silent tank. "So what am I taking tonight?"

"Everything," Mr Gilley barked. "It's taking too long to snatch the fish and scan them one at a time."

The Tie-Pin Man's eyes widened. "How are we supposed to catch them all?"

"We're going to drain the tank and take anything big enough to have swallowed the memory stick," said Mr Gilley grimly, "and cut it open."

Tie-Pin Man looked awkward. "I feel bad about all those fish," he muttered. "I thought I could just steal the technology and hand it over to you to sell."

Five figures stepped out from their hiding place on the rocky island in the middle of the tank, taking up positions on a partially submerged ledge.

"Mr Gilley," said Jo as the security man and his accomplice goggled at them, "you don't seem very reliable with your security tapes."

"So we made sure we got our own," Dylan added, holding up his videocamera.

"We figured you were in cahoots with Tie-Pin Man there," Allie put in.

"The name's Alf," interrupted the Tie-Pin Man. "I'm his brother-in-law."

Allie wiggled her fingers at him. "Hi, Alf," she

said cheerfully. "We have your tie-pin. You can wear it at your trial."

Chapter Nine

So, you kids are pretty clever after all," Mr Gilley snarled. "Too bad you won't be able to tell anyone, since you're going down the drain . . ."

He ran to the edge of the tank and turned a large valve sharply anti-clockwise. A round drain opened in the bottom of the tank – and a powerful whirlpool swept the Five off their feet and into the water.

"Whoooa!"

The water was disappearing at a terrifying speed. Taking a deep breath, Max swam down into the tank. He grabbed the deep-sea diver model and thrust it into the open drain, plugging it up.

Jo, Dylan and Allie caught their breath and trod water in the half-empty tank.

"Good work, Max – you really saved us there," Jo panted.

A big net whistled out of nowhere. It fell on the Five, trussing them up completely.

"Hey!"

"Whooahh!"

Mr Gilley started winching the net towards the deck with a nasty smile on his face. The cousins thrashed around, but it was hopeless.

"Now if you could just do something about this net, we'd really be in business," Dylan panted at Max.

Unfortunately, Max couldn't think of anything. Which is how the Five ended up tied to a row of wooden barrels lined up across the deck.

Mr Gilley and Alf winched in a net load of fish from the half-empty tank, using a crane and a nearby lorry. The fish slithered out of the net and into the lorry. The crane and net winched back for its next load.

Max thrashed around, determined to free himself from the ropes that tied him to his barrel. "I plugged

the drain," he panted stubbornly. "Someone else has to sort out this helplessly-bound-to-barrels situation."

"Actually, I think I've got a friend I can call for help . . ." said Jo suddenly. She took a deep breath. "BWAAAARAAAGH!" she bellowed.

Dylan looked shocked. "If that's your friend's name, I'm going to need help spelling it."

"BWAAARAAAGH!" Jo bellowed again.

Her voice swept through the silent aquarium, across the park and down to the amphitheatre. In its comfortable cage by the stage, the elephant seal opened its heavy-lidded eyes – and bellowed back.

"BWAAARRAAGHH!" Jo roared.

"Maybe your friend's away," Dylan suggested. His eyes widened as he saw the elephant seal flumping into view. "Oh, I'm wrong. Look out . . . !"

Bellowing with affection, the enormous seal hurled itself at Jo, landing on her and her barrel.

"Ooofff!" Jo grunted, as the seal knocked the wind out of her. She shook her head, seeing tweetie-birds in the sky.

"Are you OK, Jo?" Allie asked.

"I think so," Jo said woozily. The seal licked her

face among the ruins of the barrel and the broken ropes that now lay around her. "Yeuchh – but I smell a lot more like an elephant seal than I really care to."

Pushing the seal away, Jo loosened Dylan's ropes.

"Well, your friend deserves some sort of reward," said Dylan happily. "What do you give an elephant seal? A bathrobe? Cologne?"

The seal made a snarfing kind of sound and wobbled his belly.

"Maybe plastic surgery," Allie suggested, patting the seal gingerly. "His nose could use a little work."

Within seconds, everyone was untied. Mr Gilley and Alf were hauling in another load of fish. Their backs were turned. Seizing their chance, the Five scampered to the far side of the loaded net, running with the net as it swung towards the lorry.

"I don't think we want to say goodbye to Eely, Coddy, Sir Isaac Newton and all the other fishy guys," said Allie as they arrived at the lorry and took cover behind its front end.

"I have to agree . . ." said Max. He ran around the front of the lorry to the back of the cab. Then he

pulled the lever which controlled the dumping mechanism. As Mr Gilley and Alf dumped their next net load of fish into the lorry, the whole thing tilted up and flung its contents back towards the tank.

"Look out!" yelled Alf, backing away in horror. "Seafood!"

But it was too late. The tide of fish swept Mr Gilley and his brother-in-law back into the teeming waters of the tank.

Chapter Ten

"Woaahhhhh!"

Mr Gilley floundered to the surface of the water, fighting off the fish. He grabbed at one of the plastic temple's pillars for support. It snapped off in his hand, flinging him back down under the water.

Glaring furiously at the broken pillar in his hand, it took Mr Gilley a moment to see the little memory stick wedged under the base of the pillar. His eyes lit up. Grabbing the device, he swam back up to the surface.

"Alf!" he roared at his accomplice, waving the stick in the air in triumph. "I've got it! Let's get out of here before . . ."

A long-handled fish-net plummeted down and neatly swept the stick out of Mr Gilley's hand.

"Heyyy!" Mr Gilley wailed, staring at his empty palm.

"Before you lose it again?" Allie enquired, flipping the memory stick out of the net and catching it. "Oops! Too late."

The octopus seized the villains with two of its tentacles, immobilizing them completely.

"We phoned Constable Stubblefield," Max called down. "She'll be popping by with bath towels. Oh, and handcuffs."

Jo patted Timmy's head. On her other side, the elephant seal sidled up hopefully. Smiling, Jo petted it with her free hand. The Five stood with their arms round each other and watched the two villains still plunging helplessly about in the tank.

"You know, they could end up being the most popular attraction here," Jo grinned. "I always thought they looked a little fishy."

A few days later, the Five were back at the aquarium. This time, they were definitely there for fun.

They watched through the plate-glass wall in the underground viewing tunnel as the octopus swam around and the sea turtle glided about munching on kelp.

Max pressed his face to the glass. "Now that I can see the octopus swimming around . . . he's really not that interesting . . ." he admitted.

Shrugging, the Five left the viewing tunnel and headed up to the deck for some fresh air.

"Now, a giant crocodile – that would be brilliant," said Max thoughtfully. "Chomp!"

On the far side of the deck, a little boy pointed

at Dylan and giggled. "Look – it's the Wobbly Boy!" he squeaked to his friend. "From the internet! Hey, Wobbly Boy!"

Dylan looked surprised as the two boys started copying Dylan's thrashing, squirming dance from the time he'd had the fish down his back. He glanced at his cousins and raised puzzled eyebrows.

"We thought you wanted to be famous," Jo smirked. "So we posted the video of you with fish in your shirt on the internet."

"Do your silly dance, Wobbly Boy!" the little boy shrieked in delight.

Several interested onlookers gathered around.

"I don't remember what I did," Dylan protested, lifting his hands and backing away.

"I can take care of that," Jo said. She took a fish from a nearby feeding bucket and dropped it down Dylan's back. Instantly, Dylan broke into his Wobbly Boy routine.

"Yay!" cheered the little boy.

Pulling Dylan's hat off his madly bobbing head, Jo held it out to the crowd. Coins started raining down.

"Like you said," Jo grinned as the others burst out

laughing and joined in the dance with the thrashing Dylan. "Fifty pence is fifty pence . . ."

Epilogue

Dylan took the videocamera and pointed it at Jo, who was standing in the garden with Timmy.

"Sticky Situation Number Seventy," Dylan announced. "You Have to Train an Animal."

Jo knelt next to Timmy, helping him lie down. "To teach Timmy how to roll over," she said to the camera, "I give him a command in a firm, confident voice – 'Roll over, Timmy!' "

She helped Timmy roll on to his other side.

"And I show him how to do it," Jo continued. "Then I praise him and love him." She nuzzled Timmy's neck and tickled his tummy. "Good dog! Good Timmy!"

Timmy panted happily. Then he rolled over all on his own.

"Good boy!" said Jo in delight. "Maybe he can even have a treat."

She crossed the garden to a small table, where there was a box of dog biscuits. She peered inside the box. It was empty.

Dylan panned the camera across to where Max was sitting nearby. Max gazed into the lens, his mouth full and his hand in a bowl of dog biscuits.

"These are really good," he said in a muffled voice. "Crunchy."

"Roll over, Max!" Jo commanded.

Max dropped out of his chair and rolled over, panting happily. He really did make a good dog.